Happy Birthday to

Good Books™

Intercourse, PA 17534

800/762-7171 • www.goodbks.com

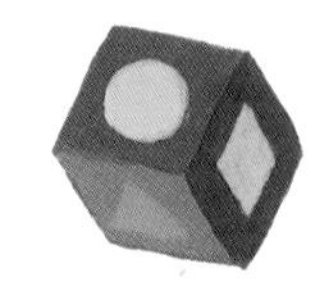

Text by Lois Rock

Original edition published in English under the title
Now You Are 1 by Lion Publishing, plc, Oxford, England.

North American edition published by Good Books, 2002.

NOW YOU ARE 1

International Standard Book Number: 1-56148-394-X
Library of Congress Catalog Card Number: 2002024140

Printed and bound in Singapore.

Library of Congress Cataloging-in-Publication Data

Rock, Lois
Now you are 1 / Lois Rock, Gabriella Buckingham.
p. cm.
Originally published: Oxford, England : Lion Pub., 2002.
Summary: One-year-olds spend their birthdays pulling things down, making noise with pots and pans, looking around themselves, smiling, waving, and sleeping.
ISBN 1-56148-394-X
[1. Birthdays--Fiction. 2. Babies--Fiction. 3. Stories in rhyme.] I. Title: Now you are one. II. Buckingham, Gabriella. III. Title.
PZ8.3.R58615 N1 2002
[E]--dc21 2002024140

Last year, little baby,
you had only just begun...

Now you've grown so strong
and tall, oh, baby:

you are

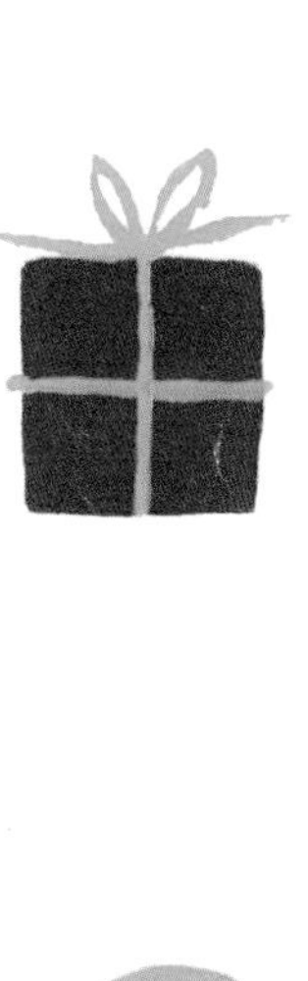

Here's a birthday
message from
the golden shining sun:
welcome to another year
of happiness and fun.

Now you are 1,
it is the time
to step and walk,
to reach and climb.

Now you are 1,
my little love,
don't pull things down
from up above.

Think of the music
you can make
with a kitchen pan
for a drum:
it is your finest
work to date –
your symphony
number 1.

Do you ever wonder
(as I often do) why people
invented the spoon,

when food's so appealing
for touching and feeling,
that *breakfast*
can last until noon?

1 little mouth

1 little nose

2 little ears

10 little toes

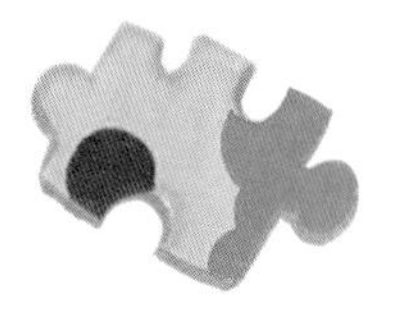

Close your eyes tight:
the world goes away.

Open them wide:
it comes back to play.

Now you are 1
you can learn all the names
of everything you can see:

a dog

and a cat

and a wiggly worm

a bird and a bumblebee...

Just think
of the words
you can learn
to say

to tell of the
things you do.

But always remember the words

you first learned, especially...

I love you.

When you're feeling
weary and you want
to rest your head

you can snuggle
with a cuddle
in your own small bed.

The angels love you,
and so do I;
they watch from heaven;
I watch close by.